W9-CZS-068

DIARY OF A MINECRAFT ZOMBIE

BOOK 1

A SCARE OF A DARE

Koala Books
An imprint of Scholastic Australia Pty Limited
PO Box 579 Gosford NSW 2250
ABN 11 000 614 577
www.scholastic.com.au

Part of the Scholastic Group
Sydney • Auckland • New York • Toronto • London • Mexico City
New Delhi • Hong Kong • Buenos Aires • Puerto Rico

First published by Zack Zombie Publishing in 2015.
Published by Scholastic Australia in 2016.
Text copyright © Zack Zombie Publishing 2016.

All rights reserved. No part of this publication may be reproduced
or transmitted in any form or by any means, electronic or
mechanical, including photocopying, recording, storage in an
information retrieval system, or otherwise, without the prior
written permission of the publisher, unless specifically permitted
under the Australian Copyright Act 1968 as amended.

This unofficial novel is an original work of fan fiction which is not
sanctioned nor approved by the makers of Minecraft. Minecraft is a
registered trademark of, and owned by, Mojang Synergies AB, and its
respective owners, which do not sponsor, authorize, or endorse this book.
All characters, names, places, and other aspects of the game described
herein are trademarked and owned by their respective owners.
Minecraft®/TM & © 2009-2021 Mojang.

 A catalogue record for this
book is available from the
National Library of Australia

ISBN 978-1-74381-150-4

Typeset in Agent ́C ́ and Potato Cut TT

Printed in China by Hang Tai Printing Company Limited.

Scholastic Australia's policy, in association with Hang Tai Printing Company, is to
use papers that are renewable and made efficiently from wood grown in responsibly
managed forests, so as to minimise its environmental footprint.

23 24 25 / 2

DIARY OF A MINECRAFT ZOMBIE

BOOK 1

A SCARE OF A DARE

BY
Zack Zombie

Koala Books

This is me, Zombie

MNDAY

'Uuuuurrrgghhhh!!!'

'Honey, it's time to get up!'

'Uuuurrrgghhhaacckkhuhh?'

'Honey, it's night-time already.
You need to get up!'

'Aww, Mum, do I have to?'

'Yes, you do. Those Villagers aren't
going to scare themselves.'

'UUUURRGGHHHHH!!!'

'Don't Uuuurrgghhhhh me. You get up and get ready, this instant!'

'Okay, Mum.'

Zombie parents can be **A REAL PAIN** sometimes. It's always, *do this* and *scare that*. Some days I wish I were Human so I wouldn't have to get up at night and go scaring. I'm sure Human parents aren't like this, always telling their kids what to do. Human parents are probably really nice and let their kids stay up all day and do whatever they want.

Not like Zombie parents.

'Don't go out during the day because you'll burn yourself! Blah, blah, blah,' they say.

One day, I'm going to stay out all day, just to see what will happen.

My friend Creepy stays out during the day and nothing happens to *him*. As a matter of fact, so does Slimey next door... **URRGGGHHHH!** They have all the fun. Why can't my parents be like that?

Well, at least I'm not alone. My best friend Skelee can't go out during the day, either. His parents are really strict. Skelee's parents won't even let him have a Dog. He said his uncle got a Dog once, but it **BURIED HIS GRANDMOTHER** in the backyard.

And they never found her.

Bummer...

TUESDAY

Well, it's a scare day today, so I have to go out and scare some Villagers again. Most of the time it's boring, but sometimes it can be fun.

One time, I crept up behind a Villager and put my arms out in front of me and said, **"UURRRGGHHH!!!"**

It really scared him.

Actually, he was so scared he ran

away and dropped his Sword. I
took it as a souvenir. Now I have
it hanging up on my wall.

Check out
my Sword!

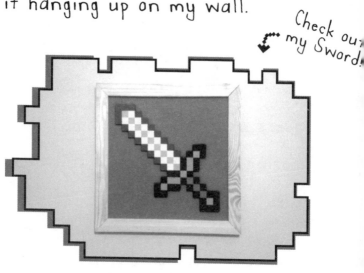

Another time, I was in a friendly
mood, and I said, 'Hi!' to a Villager.
He fainted. I think it was my
breath. Mum always tells me not
to brush my teeth. But today I
forgot and did anyway.

WEDNESDAY

There's a Zombie at school that really gets on my nerves. No, really, he steps on the nerves on my feet every time he walks by. His name is Jeff. I wouldn't be so mad if he wasn't bragging all the time.

'I scared five Villagers yesterday,' he said, really loud and in my face.

I looked at Jeff, annoyed. 'WHO CARES? Anybody can do that.'

'Well, I did it during the daytime!'

'What?! **DURING THE DAYTIME?!**'

'Yep, during the daytime!'

Either he was lying or Jeff was not such a lame-brain after all.

He said that his uncle took him out on a rainy day and they scared a bunch of Villagers that were huddled under a tree. I still don't believe him. But it would explain why he smells funny. Everyone knows that Zombies aren't supposed to get wet.

At Scare School today, the teacher taught us about the best time and place to scare Villagers. He said if we're really lucky we could catch a Villager trying to mine at night.

Miners are great because they always drop cool stuff you can take home. My buddy Creepy said his uncle scared a Miner one night. He almost went home with a big, fat Diamond.

But his uncle got so excited that he **BLEW UP.**

THURSDAY

After Scare School, me, Creepy, Skelee and Slimey like to go out to have fun. Sometimes we go to the village to cause a bit of trouble. One game we like playing is to bang on random doors and run away. I **ALMOST GOT CAUGHT** once. But I just said, 'Uuurrrrgghhh' to talk my way out of it.

Worked like a charm.

Creepy told me that he came face-to-face with a Villager once. He got so nervous he started shaking. He tried to introduce himself, but the guy just ran away. I don't think people really get Creepy like I do.

My favourite game is hide-and-seek. Our friend Slimey told us he used to play hide-and-seek with his uncle. One time his uncle hid in the water. They never heard from him again.

Slimey's uncle is in here somewhere

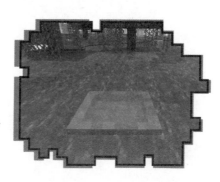

FRIDAY

Today I got home from school and my little brother started bothering me again. He's such a little anklebiter!

My little brother riding his Chicken ↘

No, really. He likes to bite my ankles and run away ... **REALLY FAST!**

Sometimes he hops on his Chicken and then I can never catch him. Mum says I used to do the same thing when I was his age. I guess they didn't feed us enough when we were kids.

My mum said I had to get ready for dinner. I asked her, 'What's for dinner tonight?'

'ROTTEN MEATLOAF,' she replied.

'Can't we go out to eat?' I asked her.

'There are no Villagers out tonight. So, no, we can't!'

Bummer. I was really hungry...

I know what you're thinking, but we don't actually eat Villagers. What happens is, when we scare them, they sometimes drop really yummy food.

One time, I scared a Villager and she **DROPPED A CAKE!** That was the best day ever.

I was so
happy when
I picked up
this cake
↳

SATURDAY

Today, Mum says we're going to my cousin's house. He lives in **THE NETHER.** It wouldn't be so bad if it wasn't so hot there all the time.

My cousin's name is Piggy. Funny name, right? Piggy doesn't think so...

When I asked Piggy where he came from, he told me something about his dad being struck by lightning or something like that. Piggy is always making crazy stuff up.

Piggy's house is right in the middle of the Nether. The Nether is a

My cousin, Piggy

nice place to visit, but I wouldn't
want to live there. The first time
I visited, I brought my sleeping
bag to make a bed. I rolled it out
to get ready to go to sleep and...
BOOM! I'm never going to do
that again.

It's also really noisy there—too
much snorting and wailing. Mum
tells me it's just the Ghasts that
do a fly-by once in a while. They're
really noisy for flying Octopuses.

Piggy introduced me to his friend
Blaze. I tried to give him a high

five, but he didn't have any hands!

Talk about awkward!

Piggy's
friend,
Blaze

Piggy and I play all kinds of games. But the only game we can't play is tag. As soon as I tag Piggy, all of his relatives get mad and start chasing me for some reason.

SUNDAY

Contrary to what most people think, Humans can be friendly.

I actually have a Human friend. His name is **STEVE**. We have a lot in common.

Steve is kind of weird looking. He has a square head and purple eyes. Steve also never changes his clothes. And I thought only Zombies did that!

Steve walks funny, too. I tried

walking like
him once, and a
Villager started
talking to me.
I didn't know
what to do, so
I ran away.
Even though he's
weird, Steve is still my friend.

Steve is my
Human friend

My mum says I shouldn't make
friends with Humans. She says
they smell funny. Plus, she says,
'If the Humans become our friends,
who are we going to scare?'

She didn't like my idea about

scaring little brothers instead
of Humans.

My mum doesn't like me asking
her too many questions.

One day I asked her, 'Mum, where
do Zombies come from?' She seemed
a bit **TONGUE-TIED.** But
then I remembered she doesn't
have a tongue anymore!

When she finally thought of
something, she said, 'Zombies
are mobs created by computer

programmers at Mojang to make the game of Minecraft a more challenging and enjoyable experience.'

Whenever my mum uses big words to answer my questions, I know she's hiding something or making it up.

My friend Creepy said that Zombies come from being bitten by other infected Zombies, who caught a plague that originated from some **SECRET MILITARY EXPERIMENT.** I think Creepy watches too much television.

I liked Skelee's answer the best.
He says Zombies aren't made—
they're born. He said they hatch
from eggs. His theory kind of
makes sense. I've seen a lot of
eggs around here.

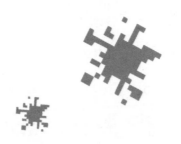

M✹NDAY

Sometimes, after school, me and the guys go out to mess with the Spiders. They don't do much. They just crawl around. But we like to tip them over. I saw some Humans do that to a Cow once. It looked like fun.

You need to **BE CAREFUL** with Cave Spiders, though. They get really mad if you tip them over. They think they're better than regular Spiders.

I found out the hard way
that you shouldn't tip over a
SILVERFISH. They travel in
gangs. It wasn't much fun getting
beaten up by Silverfish.

TUESDAY

I like the Endermen. They're really nice. They're also really tall for teenagers.

I still can't understand what they do all night, though. I guess moving blocks around is fun. But I just don't get it.

An Enderman

It's probably a secret club, and only the coolest kids can be a part of it. I tried talking to one to find out the inside scoop. It didn't work.

He just stared at me.

I wish I could travel like Endermen. They don't have to walk. They just **TELEPORT** wherever they want to go. If I could do that, I would teleport to Grandma's house every day. She always has the best snacks. My favourite is when she makes lady fingers...

...the sandwiches, I mean.

WEDNESDAY

We have a Witch that lives on our street. I think she's funny looking. She has a big nose with a mole on it. She walks around mad all the time. I would be mad too if

I had a big nose with a mole on it.

One day Skelee asked the Witch what it's

The Witch ⤴

like to have a big nose with a mole on it. She just walked away, mad.

The kids in the neighbourhood sometimes **TEASE HER** and say she's ugly. Mum says the Witch probably looked better when she was younger.

So me and the guys decided to look up her yearbook in the school library to find out...

Nope, she's always looked like that!

I wonder what it's like to have a nose. Dad says I had an uncle who had a nose. He got a cold once. And that's the last time they ever saw his nose again.

Dad also said that I had another uncle who had ears. He couldn't find them after he started wearing a helmet.

THURSDAY

I used to feel embarrassed when my body parts occasionally fell off. Now, I've realised it's the best excuse ever for staying home from school!

It doesn't happen often. But when it does, I milk it for all it's worth. I just have to pick the right body parts.

One time, I said, 'Mum, I just **LOST AN EYEBALL!**'

'CONGRATULATIONS

honey!' she said.

But now, I stick to the legs. You can't go to school without legs.

Mum says that when a Zombie loses a tooth, they can put it under their pillow and the tooth fairy will come and give you a dollar.

I thought I had struck it rich, until I realised that the most I can ever make is three dollars.

FRIDAY

Mum and Dad said that if I get good marks on my Scare test, I can get a pet.

That sounded awesome until I realised I could only get a pet Squid. I would rather have a Cat or a Dog, like Steve does. But Mum says we can't because we shed all over the furniture.

'Dogs have a habit of burying our **BODY PARTS** in the backyard,' she says.

'Cats are worse. They have a habit of turning everything into a scratching post.'

Squids are okay, I guess. But all they do is swim around.

Creepy's parents gave him a Pig. Now that's a **COOL PET.**

He didn't have it for long, though. One day it got struck by lightning. Then my cousin Piggy thought he saw it roaming around his neighbourhood in the Nether.

Creepy's uncle

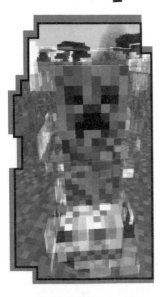

Speaking of lightning, one of Creepy's uncles got struck by lightning once. They took him to the hospital.

He didn't stay long, though, because the

HOSPITAL EXPLODED.

I think the Witch on our street was struck by lightning once, too. It probably hit her on the nose.

I guess if I got struck by lightning, I'd be mad too.

SATURDAY

My uncle Wither is coming to visit today. I wouldn't mind, but he usually makes such a mess!

I tried sneaking up on him once. I couldn't do it. He seems to always know when I'm coming.

I'm not going to be able to stay long, though. I want to go see Skelee's older brother's new band. They call themselves The **WALKING DEAD.**

Cool.

Mum doesn't like them. She says they're a **BAD INFLUENCE.** She says if I keep listening to music like that I'll start acting more Human.

Uncle Wither told me he was in a band once. I thought it was a rock band. Turned out it was Obsidian.

Not cool.

☀ SUNDAY ☀

I thought I would go visit Steve today. Steve sometimes likes to mine at night. Sometimes I try to creep up on him and scare him. But he usually hears me coming.

Steve says he wants to be a Zombie like me. He says **ZOMBIES** have the easy life.

Boy, if he only knew...

I tried to introduce Steve to my friends. But Creepy got really nervous around him. So we had to put Creepy in a timeout.

Steve and Skelee got along really well. They even played Cowboys and Indians. Steve is usually the Cowboy. I know because when they're finished, Steve's usually **COVERED IN ARROWS.**

Today Steve asked me how you can tell a girl Zombie from a boy Zombie.

I said, 'That's easy. All you have to do is look at our clothes.'

Steve just looked at me, confused.

Maybe it's because all Zombies' clothes look the same to Humans.

Then he asked me if Zombies had **GIRLFRIENDS.**

'Yeah, they do,' I said.

Then he asked me if I had a Zombie girlfriend.

I said, 'Of course I do! What do you think I am, a loser?'

The truth is, I don't have a girlfriend. But Sally Cadaver, from Biology Class, has been in each of my classes since second grade, so

she's the closest thing I've ever
had to a girlfriend.

'**HOW DO YOU KISS,**
since you don't have lips?' Steve
asked.

I didn't know what to say, so I
just looked at Steve with my best
blank stare.

M✳NDAY

A few weeks ago a new kid transferred to my school. His name is Jake. He's a Wither Skeleton.

This is Jake ⤳

They say he got kicked out of his last school because he **POISONED** somebody.

I think I'm going to make friends with him so that if anyone messes with me, Jake could threaten to poison them too. I just hope he doesn't poison me first. Either way, it's always good to have someone like Jake on your side.

You see, being a Zombie in school can be a dangerous thing. Sometimes you need protection. Especially from bullies.

The biggest bully in school is a kid named **MIKE MAGMA.** He's a Magma Cube. Everybody says he's a real hot-head. What's weird is that Mike is Slimey's cousin, and he picks on Slimey, too.

I wonder what kind of poison Jake would use on Mike Magma.

Well, a kid can dream, can't he?

 TUESDAY

Today the class went to a new village to practise scaring. I was a little nervous because Jeff said this village had an **IRON GOLEM.**

If you don't know what an Iron Golem is, just imagine a giant foot designed for the sole purpose of squashing a Zombie like a Cockroach.

Jeff said no Zombie had ever seen one and lived to tell the tale.

'Do they know who it was?' I
asked.

'Nope.'

'What's wrong with you, anyway?'
Skelee asked.

'Just a cold,' I said, as I slowly
COVERED MY HANDS.

SATURDAY

After my miraculous one-day recovery, Dad decided to take me on a camping trip.

The Swamp Biome

He wanted to take me to the Swamp Biome. He said the stale air would do me some good. Dads like to take their kids on camping

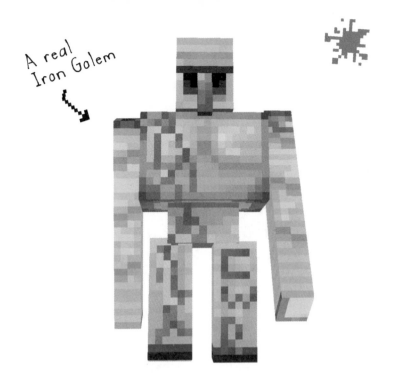

A real Iron Golem

Our teacher, Ms Bones, heard our conversation and told us that there were no Iron Golems at the village.

Still, I like my limbs, and I would like to keep them, thank you.

When we got there, Creepy got nervous and started shaking again. Ms Bones decided to send him home with a note.

The village was actually quite **PEACEFUL.** There were no Villagers out so I practised scaring some Sheep.

The Sheep I tried to scare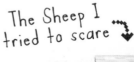

It didn't work very well.

They just stood there looking at me.

WEDNESDAY

Today I got caught passing a note
to Skelee in class.

It wouldn't be so bad if today
wasn't the day that Skelee
wanted to know **WHO I LIKED.**
And it wouldn't be so bad if we had
one of those laid-back, nice teachers.

Not Ms Bones, though. She is as
stiff as they come. She has a rule
that if she catches anyone passing
notes in her class, she reads them

out loud to everybody.

And today, she read my note out loud: 'I LIKE SALLY CADAVER AND I WANT HER TO BE MY GIRLFRIEND.'

My life is **OFFICIALLY OVER** . . .

The only thing that saved me was that Sally was out for the week because she was getting her tonsils put back in.

But now the whole school knows! Including Jeff. Knowing Jeff, he's going to try to beat me at getting Sally as a girlfriend.

Ever since we were kids, Jeff has always tried to show that he's better than me at something.

Jeff was the first to lose his baby teeth... and his regular teeth.

Jeff was the first to grow mould on his chest.

Jeff was also the first to get a Villager to faint during scare practice.

It wouldn't be so bad, but Jeff is

better looking than me too. He's lost more hair than I have.

He's a nicer shade of green than I am. And he's got more of his guts and entrails showing than I do.

Will Jeff always beat me at everything?

He'll get Sally Cadaver to be his girlfriend in no time.

I'M DOOMED.

☀ THURSDAY ☀

After what happened yesterday, I decided to fake being sick to stay home from school.

Usually a missing limb would do the trick, but I think my mum and dad were on to me.

So I decided to use the trick up my sleeve...

I was going to **TAKE A BATH!**

Zombies are not supposed to get

wet. And Zombies are definitely not supposed to take baths! It takes a lot of years to get your rotting flesh just the right colour and smell.

Taking a bath would make you look like you were *The Living*. Exactly the effect I wanted.

Mum and Dad didn't know that I knew about baths. I learned it from Steve. He says Humans take baths all the time. That would explain why Mum says that Humans **SMELL FUNNY.**

So, right before evening, when the moon was about to rise, I woke up early, snuck out of the house and ran to the lake.

This is it, I thought.

As I was looking at the lake, and getting myself ready to jump in, **OLD MAN JENKINS** came up, riding his Zombie Horse.

'What do you think you're doing, young man?'

'I'm about to take a bath!' I said.

'What on the **OVERWORLD** would you do that for?'

So, I told him the whole story. As weird as it was, I could tell he knew from first-hand experience what I was going through. I guess all Zombies have to go through this stuff as kids.

Then Old Man Jenkins said, 'Just wash your hand and tell your mum and dad you caught a rash at school. Always used to work for me.'

So I tried it... and it worked like a charm! I got to spend the whole day at home.

Now I just have to find another way to stay home from school tomorrow.

FRIDAY

Today I washed the other hand and told my mum and dad that the rash had spread. Luckily, they believed it.

The only problem is, they believed it so much that they started to worry about me. My mum and dad rushed me to the hospital so that the doctor could check to see if I was **TURNING HUMAN.** They even called a specialist to see if I was contagious.

Great, not only do the kids at school think I'm an outcast, the whole neighbourhood will too, I thought.

The specialist was a **WITCH DOCTOR** from the Swamp Biome. I didn't know that men could be Witches too. But there he was, with a big nose that had a mole on it and everything.

After checking me over, he sent me home. I think the Witch Doctor knew I was faking. Probably because he had to do the same thing when he was a kid.

Later on, Skelee, Creepy and Slimey came over to see how I was doing. Creepy was so nervous about catching what I had, that he started **SHAKING** again. The guys sent him home because the pressure was too much for him.

I asked the guys how it went at school.

'They sent everyone home because some kid at school caught the "White Hand" disease.'

trips, thinking that they will do them good.

Slimey's dad took him to the Snowy Biome once. I don't think he thought it through, though. They were **FROZEN SOLID** for a few days until they were discovered by some tourists.

Skelee's dad took him to the Forest Biome. Afterwards, he said he wasn't expecting there to be so many Wolves.

Creepy's dad took him and the whole family on a field trip to the

Desert Biome. Nobody warned them about the Cactuses.

Now, I'm not saying dads don't mean well. It's just that they don't have a great track record when it comes to preparing for these trips.

Mums, on the other hand, prepare for everything. My mum even gave me some bug spray so that the swamp bugs would **LAY EGGS ON ME** on my trip.

Dad didn't think of that.

☀ SUNDAY ❊

Today I went to go visit Steve.

When I saw him, he was busy punching a tree.

Steve punching a tree. He's weird sometimes ↘

I was going to ask him what he

was doing, but I'm used to seeing him do weird things like that.

I must have looked at him funny, because Steve asked, 'What's eating you?'

'**MAGGOTS.** How about you?' I replied.

'No, I mean what's bothering you?' he said.

So I told him the whole story about Sally Cadaver.

'Wow, Zombies and Humans aren't

very different,' Steve said.

'We smell different.'

'Yeah, that's true,' Steve said.
'But on the inside, we're exactly
the same.'

I just looked at Steve, confused.
Didn't he know that I was missing
HALF MY INSIDES?

Steve smiled and went back to
punching his tree.

I went home and I decided that I wanted to test how strong I was. I was going to show Jeff that I could do anything he could.

So, I decided to go out during the day. Creepy's coming with me to take pictures, so I can prove I did it.

Hey, if Steve could punch a tree... I could do this!

MONDAY

All my skin burned off when I went in the sun!

Stayed home from school today to grow my skin back after I went out in the sun.

OUCH.

TUESDAY

Back to school today.

I was bummed because I wanted to skip another day of school. But rotten flesh grows back pretty fast.

I guess it's **NOT SO BAD,** because today we're going on an excursion.

Excursions can be hit-and-miss sometimes, though.

Ms Bones took us to an abandoned mine once. It was cool, but Skelee got lost and we couldn't find him for days. He said he got kidnapped by some blood-thirsty humans that wanted to **EAT HIS BRAINS.**

But I think he just got stuck in a Spider web and was too embarrassed to tell anyone.

Especially since Skelee doesn't have blood or a brain.

Ms Bones said that we were taking a trip to the Ender World. That's where **THE ENDERMEN** live. This is great because I can finally settle a bet with Slimey over what an Enderman house looks like.

Slimey says it's probably a castle made of Obsidian and Diamonds. I think it's probably more like a junkyard since they are always picking up blocks of stuff.

Ms Bones said we may even see the Ender Dragon. That would be so cool.

I've heard about the Ender Dragon. It's supposed to be this awesome dragon that flies around in the **ENDER WORLD.**

My dad said that he saw it fly by once. But I think my dad made that up just to look cool. I think the older you get, the harder dads work at trying to be cool.

WEDNESDAY

The excursion yesterday was a total flop.

Nobody told me that it was an excursion to the Ender World Natural Museum. It's just like teachers to ruin a kid's dream.

The only Enderman I met was the security guard that was guarding the **ENDER CRYSTAL** exhibit.

We didn't even get to see the Ender Dragon. But I have to admit, the Ender Dragon exhibit was pretty awesome. They only had a **SKELETON** of the Ender Dragon, but it was huge! Skelee was drooling.

☀ THURSDAY ☀

After class today, I saw Sally Cadaver. She was talking to that big-mouth Jeff.

I wanted to say hi, and see if I could take my relationship with her to the next level. But Jeff started bragging again before I could talk to her.

'I saw an Iron Golem with my uncle yesterday!' he said.

'**BIG DEAL,**' I said.

I knew I had to step up my game, or my feeble chances of making Sally want to be my girlfriend would be **UTTERLY CRUSHED.**

'Yeah, well... I actually touched one!' I said.

Mouths opened. Books dropped. I heard creaking noises as heads turned towards me.

Oh man. I had really stepped in it now.

I knew the next words out

of Jeff's mouth were going
to determine the fate of my
existence for all eternity.

'**I DARE YOU** to do it again!'
Jeff said.

He said it! I was doomed.

'Okay,' I said, thinking that I
might have just enough time to
get out of town.

But Sally looked at me like I was
the Ender Dragon himself. So of
course I had to open my big mouth
and say, 'When and where. Just

name it!'

'I'll show you where. Tomorrow night,' Jeff said.

Great, I have one day left to live...

FRIDAY

Today is the day.

Today is the day I face my death at the hands of an Iron Golem.

The Iron
Golem

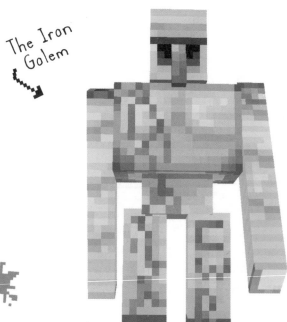

I went downstairs and gave my mum and dad a **FAREWELL HUG.** They didn't know that today would be my last day to live, but I didn't have the heart to tell them.

My little brother was riding his Chicken around too fast so I didn't get a chance to say goodbye to him either.

After school, Jeff had his uncle take us to where they saw the Iron Golem before.

And sure enough, there it was, standing guard in front of the village. Everybody from school was there, too.

Great, I'm gonna die, and there's gonna be an audience, I thought.

My family's name will be cursed forever.

There was **SALLY**, looking at me through her big eye sockets, so proud of the Zombie that I had become.

Well, at least she can enjoy it for

the next few short minutes of my
life, I thought.

'Okay, it's time,' Jeff said.

GULP! Well, here goes nothing.

I started walking towards the
Iron Golem. As I started walking,
it looked at me and got into a
Zombie-squashing stance.

'Oh man, this is going to hurt,' I
said, under my breath.

My dad told me that when he
was in the Zombie Army, he got

hit by an Iron Golem once. He said it took them weeks to find his left arm and leg. All this for Sally Cadaver. Man, girls are just trouble!

I was just about within arm's reach of the Iron Golem when I thought to myself, *This is dumb. Who am I kidding? I'm a loser.*

I started to turn around in utter shame when all of a sudden **STEVE** jumped out from behind the Iron Golem.

The crowd went silent.

Then Steve came over to me and put his arm around my shoulder, and walked me to the Iron Golem. The Iron Golem lifted up his hand like he planned to crush the both of us with a single blow...

Then when his hand came down, it was **FULL OF FLOWERS!**

He gave them to me and Steve, and I took some.

The crowd was so surprised, I think some of them literally dropped their jaws.

I walked back to the crowd of mobs and handed the flowers to Sally. Everybody started cheering.

I turned around and gave Steve a **THUMBS UP.**

And he gave me one back.

Steve gave me a thumbs up

SATURDAY

Yesterday was the best day ever.

I survived being almost crushed by an Iron Golem. I proved to Jeff that I am better at something than he is. And **SALLY CADAVER,** the closest thing I've had to a girlfriend, is now my girlfriend!

But I still wish someone would tell me how I'm supposed to kiss her with no lips.

Everybody is talking about what happened yesterday, too.

But the thing that people are really talking about is how I have a Human friend named Steve. Guess the **SECRET'S OUT.**

Well, I hope more Zombies can find friends like Steve. Then, instead of going out scaring Villagers at night, we could all just get along.

Even though he's Human, I still like Steve

SUNDAY

Today, Steve invited me to come visit his village.

I'm going to bring Skelee, Creepy and Slimey with me. I think it's going to be a lot of fun.

Creepy was a little scared, though. I had to calm him down. I don't know why he's so scared.

I mean really... **WHAT COULD GO WRONG?**